This book belongs to

_____

This edition published by Parragon Books Ltd in 2016

Parragon Books Ltd
Chartist House
15–17 Trim Street
Bath BA1 1HA, UK
www.parragon.com

ISBN 978-1-4748-4472-7

Printed in Poland

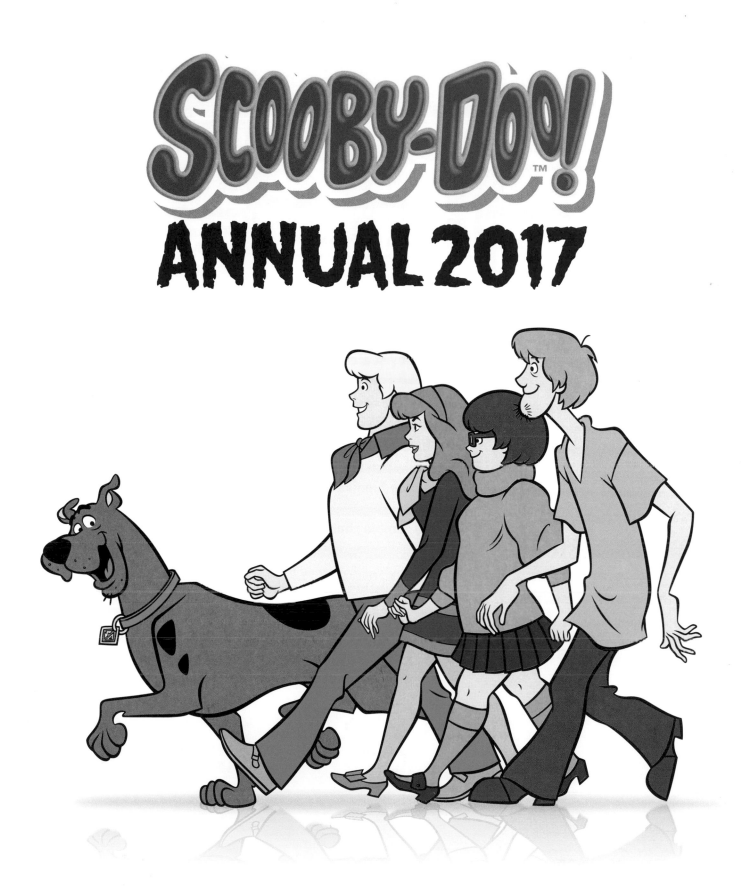

SCOOBY-DOO!™
ANNUAL 2017

PaRragon

Bath • New York • Cologne • Melbourne • Delhi
Hong Kong • Shenzhen • Singapore

CONTENTS

MEET THE GANG!
SHAGGY AND SCOOBY

Best friends Scooby-Doo and Shaggy Rogers are rarely apart. They both have big appetites and a mutual love for Scooby Snacks. They are also very easily spooked!

Spot eight Scooby Snacks hidden around these pages before they're all eaten up!

When she's not losing her glasses, Velma Dinkley is the brains of the group. Happiest when solving a tough mystery, her favourite catchphrase is 'Jinkies!'

Fashion-loving Daphne Blake is known for her trademark red hair, purple dress and green scarf. When solving mysteries she often lands the gang in danger. Her nickname is 'danger-prone Daphne'!

DAPHNE AND VELMA

Fred Jones is leader of the gang and driver of the Mystery Machine. He's very brave and often splits everyone up to search for important clues.

The Mystery Machine takes the gang all over the world on their spooky adventures. It's bright and colourful and is packed full of useful equipment which helps the gang out of some seriously spook-tastic scrapes!

FRED AND THE MYSTERY MACHINE

The story continues on page 20.

SKETCH SCOOBY

Using a pen or pencil, copy the picture of Scooby on the left into the big grid below. Draw him square by square, until you have your very own hungry Great Dane.

SCOOBY-DOOBY-DOO!

HEAD IN THE CLOUDS

Jinkies! Our clumsy canine has kicked over a barrel of flour. Can you help us find the words lost in the cloud?

```
R S S V R H B A A H F F I E
L I L E O D S O N V Q C V I
O J X C B H C K L A X C V B
R A O S Y H O K T K S A E K
A M H S L V O M B H W X Z H
B C X R N W B R G N E P O E
M Y S T E R Y R I E S A R J
X T C L C S R E B I S B Z I
D O A S M H O T G U E T E N
S C R O S A U F O N O M L K
T W Y T D G K K M O N R T I
G I L S K G Z T H Z E K R E
C L U M S Y S R Z O I N K S
U Q A C S O R Z D E A A C R
K K L A M M I E S S G P S H
M K M A B A T S P O O K S E
D A P H N E R Z E L A M S K
E R R E A R D O U U W B E E
B K B F P C G A N G S K L C
```

- [ ] Scooby
- [ ] Daphne
- [ ] Shaggy
- [ ] Jinkies
- [ ] Zoinks
- [ ] Mystery
- [ ] Scary
- [ ] Gang
- [ ] Spooks

Can you find all nine words?

FLOUR

18

CODE BREAKERS

Help Velma, Shaggy and Scooby unlock the mystery message below by using the code on the right. Write the correct letters in the empty boxes below.

CODE
1 = A
2 = B
3 = C
4 = D
5 = E
6 = F
7 = G
8 = H
9 = I
10 = J
11 = K
12 = L
13 = M
14 = N
15 = O
16 = P
17 = Q
18 = R
19 = S
20 = T
21 = U
22 = V
23 = W
24 = X
25 = Y
26 = Z

23	1	20	3	8

15	21	20

6	15	18

20	8	5

23	15	12	6

19

Story continued from page 15.

Can you guess the type of monster
from the clues below?

Clue 1

I come from
Egypt but have
cousins in
Chile and Peru.

Clue 2

I am quite
wrapped up
in myself.

Clue 3

I moan a lot,
especially when
I'm moving.

Clue 4

I walk very
slowly and
shuffle my feet.

Clue 5

I sleep in
a tomb, usually
in a pyramid.

I am a _____

Q: Why do mummies have trouble keeping friends?
A: They're too wrapped up in themselves.

Q: Why don't mummies go on holiday?
A: They're afraid they'll relax and unwind.

Q: What did the mummy film director say when the final scene was done?
A: Okay everybody, that's a wrap!

Q: Why do mummies make excellent spies?
A: They're good at keeping things under wraps.

Mummy funnies

We've got the mummy jokes all wrapped up!

HA HA HA

RUH REE REE

TOMB OF TRIVIA

Did you know?

Bodies were placed in a coffin, and sometimes that coffin was then placed into another coffin - this time made of stone. A stone coffin is called a sarcophagus. The sarcophagus was then put into a tomb.

Freaky fact

In ancient Egypt the body of a dead king or queen was washed, prepared and wrapped in strips of cloth. But a mummy of legend becomes a living monster if it is cursed or can't stand to be without the person it loves!

Freaky fact

Even though they're not actually alive, mummies shuffle, moan and chase people around.

Did you know?

Mummies from films and stories want to rest in peace – they like their cosy, quiet tombs. But treasure hunters and scientists wake them from their sleep and make the mummies mad.

Like, a little faster, Scoob!

UURRRGGGHHHH!!

Freaky fact

In films and stories, mummies are very strong and they carry a curse that affects those who wake them. Once a battle with a mummy is over, it will return to its tomb to rest ... until the next time someone wakes it of course!

Freaky fact

Some mummies can move objects just by thinking about it - the process is called telekinesis. Others can control insects or the weather and some can even shape sand with their minds (even though they don't have a brain!).

Freaky fact

Unwrapped, the bandages of a mummy could stretch for 1.6 kilometres. JEEPERS!

Yikes!

Freaky fact

The best way to protect yourself from a mummy is with fire - mummies are afraid of It because their wrappings catch fire very easily. If you set one on fire, it will be destroyed.

Freaky fact

A mummy was filled with a stuffing so it would look like a normal body.

Scooby's SCARY Story time

Lost in the lighthouse

The sun was shining, a gentle breeze was blowing. Scooby-Doo and the gang were on their way to visit Fred's Aunt Lucy, the lighthouse keeper, and her family on Bell Bottom Island.

"Like, maybe we should have skipped that last pepperoni pizza, Scooby," Shaggy said.

"Guys," Daphne giggled. "This is the smoothest ride ever! Look at Captain Rodney's puppies."

"This boat ride is great," agreed Fred. "I can't wait to spend the night at a real lighthouse."

Velma nodded. "Most lighthouses don't have keepers anymore, everything is automated."

"Until I retired last year, I was the lighthouse keeper," Captain Rodney said. "I didn't know it at the time, but it was the best job in the world." A shadow passed over his face. "Now other people live on the island and I'm stuck driving back and forth, back and forth...."

Every time Captain Rodney said 'back and forth' he pressed the accelerator pedal, and Shaggy and Scooby turned green.

"Will this ever end?" moaned Shaggy.

"Yes!" said Fred, pointing as they rounded a bend. The lighthouse loomed ahead, dark and forbidding. Its beacon turned slowly, casting an eerie light.

"Zoinks!" said Shaggy as they docked. "Maybe we're better off on the open seas."

"Maybe you are," Uncle Lou agreed. He stepped closer, with Aunt Lucy and their kids, Luke and Lisa. "The lighthouse warns ships of danger, but there is plenty of danger right here. If I were you, I'd turn around."

"Captain Rodney!" Shaggy called.

"Raptain Rodrey!" Scooby called.

They raced to the end of the dock, tripping over fish nets. But the captain had already pulled away. They were stuck on the island.

Aunt Lucy hurried over to untangle the friends. "Don't pay attention to Uncle Lou," she told them. "There isn't any danger." She paused. "But things have been a little strange here. The lights have been going off and on and some fire-fighting equipment has gone missing."

"And what about the spooky moans!" Lisa jumped in.

"And the rats!" added Luke.

Inside the lighthouse, Aunt Lucy led the gang up a spiral staircase to the watch room.

"This is where I keep information about weather," Aunt Lucy explained, "and write notes about ships and visitors in logs."

Toys and empty milk cartons littered the floor.

"It's also our playroom," Uncle Lou said, frowning. "And my workroom. The kids and I don't have anywhere else to go."

Suddenly, thunder boomed, and the lights flickered off. Uncle Lou handed out torches.

"Nothing to worry about!" said Aunt Lucy. "Since you're visiting, I'll enter all your names into the log. 'F-r-e-d'," she wrote.

Suddenly, she dropped the pen. Thin, spidery handwriting was slowly appearing across the page, letter by letter.

"'L-E-A-V-E'," Velma read, "'W-H-I-L-E Y-O-U C-A-N'."

Shaggy gulped in fear. He ran his finger down the visitor list in horror. "And there's never been a pizza delivery to the lighthouse!"

"Good thing we're here!" said Velma. "We'll solve the mystery!"

"And order pizza?" Shaggy said hopefully.

Fred ignored him. "Here's the plan. We search the island for clues. Everyone, take a room."

Shaggy and Scooby took the lantern room, where Aunt Lucy kept extra snacks.

Inside, the light spun slowly. Like a mirror, the windows reflected Shaggy and Scooby – and a creature slinking behind them! He was big and green, with glowing eyes. A zombie!

"I am the Creeper," he snarled.

"Come on, Scoob!" Shaggy cried.

They turned and ran down the twisty staircase. Halfway down, they stopped short. Two small zombies stood on a landing, moaning loudly.

Meanwhile, the Creeper was lurching down the steps, heading towards them. "Leave this island," he growled.

"Scoob!" shouted Shaggy. "We're surrounded!"

There was nowhere for them to go but outside. Shaggy and Scooby backed out onto the widow's walk. They edged towards the very end of the deck. Suddenly, a trapdoor opened beneath them. Down they dropped, onto a soft mossy hill.

The Creeper was closing in on Shaggy and Scooby. There had to be a place to hide! Up ahead, they spied a cave.

Inside, an eerie light lit the cavern. They pressed against a wall.

Shaggy kicked something hard, and jumped. But it was only a box, addressed to Uncle Lou.

"I'll get you!" cried the Creeper, running past the entrance.

Shaggy and Scooby sighed with relief – until they felt something furry scurrying over their feet. Animals! With big teeth and long tails!

"Rats!" cried Scooby.

"Like, I hope you mean cats," Shaggy said. Shaggy and Scooby raced back inside the lighthouse.

By the light of the moon, dark and spooky shapes loomed in the hall. Scooby clutched Shaggy. "Rull!"

"Skull?" repeated Shaggy. "No, Scoob, it's just a switch, probably for a light." Scooby pressed the shape.

Whiirrr! The switch released an axe. The axe swung down, barely missing Shaggy's chin. "Aagh! Let's get out of here!" Shaggy cried.

Scooby and Shaggy ran outside and down to the end of the dock.

"We've got to get out of here," Shaggy told Fred, Daphne and Velma as he waved his arms in case Captain Rodney and his boat were nearby. "There are rats everywhere! I stubbed my toe on a box in a cave."

"Raxe, Raggy!" said Scooby.

"Oh yeah! Scooby and I almost got whacked by a fire axe!"

The rest of the gang disappeared inside the lighthouse. Meanwhile, the Creeper and the little zombies had spotted Shaggy and Scooby. Quickly, the two friends took off, running under the widow's walk.

"Ready!" called Daphne.

They sprinted past the trapdoor.

"Aim," said Velma.

Then they rushed by the cannon.

"Fire!" Daphne and Velma shouted.

Fred lit the fuse. *BOOM!* The cannon shot out a net. The net dropped, catching the Creeper and his zombie sidekicks.

Aunt Lucy rushed over. "You caught the Creeper? Thank goodness! I think those zombies got Lou and the kids!"

Velma shook her head. "Not likely," she said. "They ARE Lou and the kids."

"I don't want to live on the island anymore," Uncle Lou explained to Aunt Lucy. "So I tried to scare you into giving up your job. First, I had rats shipped to the island. Then I told Luke and Lisa to moan, and I tinkered with the electricity. When all that didn't work, I bought these costumes, and set up the fire axe." He ran his finger along the edge. "I covered it with rubber."

"What about the spooky note?" asked Aunt Lucy.

"Uncle Lou wrote 'L E-A-V-E' with the kids' milk," Velma said. "It's like invisible ink. When you turned on the torch, the words appeared."

"I can't believe you went to all that trouble to convince me to leave, especially when we have to leave anyway. The lighthouse is being automated," Aunt Lucy explained.

Just then Captain Rodney arrived.

"Saw that crazy kid waving, and came to see what's going on. I also heard you'll be moving soon. Maybe we can go into business together!" he said to Uncle Lou. "Your family can drive the boat and I can give tours of the island."

"Sounds like a plan!" said Aunt Lucy.

"Like, I've got another plan," Shaggy said. "Now that we have a boat, we can bring back –"

"Rizza!" said Scooby.

THE END

TOP TO BOTTOM

Can you help Scooby-Doo and Shaggy escape the clutches of the Creeper? Find a way from the top of the lighthouse steps to the bottom.

START

END

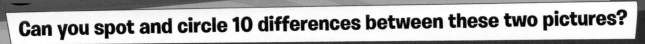

SCOOBY CHANGES

Can you spot and circle 10 differences between these two pictures?

35

SCOOBY SEARCH

```
C L U E S K D S T O K Z O A Z
L M R S S V U S B A A H A A H
R Z L I L E K A N S W E R S V
S I O H X C J E E P E R S L A
G A F R A I D H L K T K K T K
C D A W H S G V K M B H M B H
A L B C R E A T U R E D R O D
A O U X P K V O A E R Z O M S R
M I X T B E F N N T E N O E O
I Y D O Z L K G O T R M N R M
Y A S C V M D L K F O B S O B
I T A W R A G E G K W F T W F
K Y X O W S K D O X R M E R M
E A S G R O O V Y F O C R O X
S T A D R R G C G K W F K W F
```

36

CREATURE CAPTURE

Each member of the gang is hunting down a creepy villain. Follow the lines to find out who successfully captured who.

WEREWOLF

ZOMBIE

DRACULA

CLOWN

37

MONSTER MYSTERY 2

Can you guess the type of monster from the clues below?

Clue 1

I'm never happy - I moan all the time.

Clue 2

I don't like to rush - I move very, very slowly.

Clue 3

My nickname is 'the living dead'.

Rooby Rooby Roooooo!

Clue 4

Keep your distance because I stink!

I am a _____

Zombie funnies
We've got the zombie jokes sorted!

39

Voodoo zombies are quite different from other legendary zombies. In voodoo, a bokor - or sorcerer - turns people into zombies.

Fun fact

You can easily outrun a zombie - they are very slow.

A bokor fed the zombies a poisonous powder or potion which put them under his spell and made them his slaves. The zombies would then do whatever the bokor asked of them, such as attacking enemies, or carrying out curses.

In films and stories zombies are created in other ways, too. Chemicals and zombie viruses can turn humans into zombies. A single bite from a zombie can infect you and you too could become one of the walking dead!

According to legend, zombies are not affected by their surroundings - they can live anywhere, which makes them much harder to hide from. Zombies do not have any super powers either. In fact, they can do much less than they could when they were living.

Long ago, people were sometimes buried alive - doctors thought they were dead but they were only in a coma. Thieves would dig up graves to steal jewellery and often came face to face with these corpses coming back to life! Yikes!

Many people believe Frankenstein's monster is a zombie but actually he's not.... Frankenstein stitched his monster together using body parts from lots of different dead people. Unlike zombies, he could think, talk and didn't want to eat your brains like zombies do!

Fun fact

Zombies can't swim but they can't drown either.

MRRUUGGHHH!

Top tips for protecting yourself against zombies!

• Carry something noisy - if you throw it away from yourself then a zombie will follow the sound, letting you make your escape.

• Protect your body - wear leather boots to cover your legs and feet and thick leather gloves to keep your hands and fingers safe. Layers of clothing help protect you from a zombie's bite.

• Never travel on your own - you have a better chance of surviving if you are with your friends!

Fun fact

The only way to kill a zombie is to destroy its brain.

Legend says that zombies love to eat fresh meat from any living creature; birds, horses, dogs and even people! Some zombies' favourite thing to eat is human brains - **Yuck!**

Like, did you just hear a noise, Scoob?

Scooby's SCARY Story time

The mystery mansion

The Mystery Machine cruised down the road. The gang was heading towards a camp site on the beach. Above the sea, they could see dark clouds.

"Uh-oh," said Daphne, looking out of the window. "I hope those clouds aren't heading our way."

Before the gang could even set up their tent, the rain started. Within minutes, it turned into a downpour.

"Like, I'm already wet, and I haven't even put my toe in the sea yet!" said Shaggy.

Scooby shook. "Ree, roo!"

"Well, I guess we'll have to cut this camping trip short – very short," said Fred. Everyone piled back into the van and looked for some place to stay for the night. Before long, they came upon a hotel mansion high on a cliff.

Fred turned into the driveway. "Let's see if they have any rooms available," he said.

As soon as the gang walked in, the owner of the hotel rushed over.

"Welcome! Welcome!" he said. "I am Mr MacDuff. I'm so pleased to have you stay with us." He went on to explain that the hotel had been family-run for over 100 years. "But business has been so slow lately, I'm not sure how much longer I can stay open."

"That's too bad," said Velma.

Just then, Mr MacDuff called to the porter and handed him some keys. "Marty, will you show these folks to their rooms?"

Marty nodded. He led them upstairs and said, "Wow, you guys are brave."

"Brave? Why?" asked Fred.

"Well, this place is haunted," explained Marty. "That's why no one stays here anymore."

"Zoinks!" said Shaggy. "Maybe we shouldn't stay here either!"

"Don't be silly," said Fred. "Besides, in this weather, there's nowhere else to go."

Just after midnight, Shaggy, Scooby and Fred were woken up by some strange noises and scary voices.

"Get out! Get out before it's too late!" the voices said.

"Like, is it just me, or is someone trying to tell us something?" said Shaggy. "Maybe it's time to go."

The guys ran into Daphne and Velma in the hall, who had heard the same thing.

"Let's go and investigate," said Fred.

"Aw, I was afraid you'd say that," Shaggy said.

"We'll split up," suggested Fred.

"I was afraid you were gonna say that, too," said Shaggy.

"You guys check up here, and the rest of us will look downstairs," Fred said.

Shaggy gulped. "Come on, Scoob," he said. "Let's start looking. But I really, really, really hope we don't find anything!"

"Re, roo," agreed Scooby as he followed Shaggy down the hall.

The first two rooms were empty. But Scooby and Shaggy heard a terrible moaning coming from the third room. Just then the door opened and a masked figure lunged for them.

"Zoinks!" Shaggy and Scooby ran to the end of the hall.

They opened the last door on the left, ran inside and slammed it shut.

"Like, yikes!" said Shaggy. "That was a close one!"

Inside the room, the paint was peeling off the walls and all of the floorboards were broken. But the room was empty.

"Whew," said Shaggy. "All this searching is making me hungry. I think it's time for a Scooby Snack break."

Scooby eagerly agreed and plopped down on an old-looking chair. *Whump!* Scooby was launched from the chair, down through a trap door, and onto the floor below!

Luckily, Fred was on the floor below, and Scooby fell right into his arms!

Fred wasn't expecting to play catch and he lost his balance. He wobbled and fell backwards against a bookcase. *Whoosh!* The bookcase turned around. Suddenly, Fred and Scooby found themselves inside a secret lab!

Meanwhile, Velma and Daphne were checking the area around the front door. The owner was nowhere to be seen, but Velma did spot something on the floor.

"I wonder what this stuff is," Velma said, bending down and putting one finger on the purple goo. It was sticky.

"Let's go find the others and show them," said Daphne.

Daphne and Velma searched for Fred in the library, but they couldn't find him.

Suddenly they heard a howl and a "Whoooooaaa!" Before they knew it, Shaggy fell from the floor above and landed at their feet!

"Shaggy! Are you all right?" Daphne asked him.

"Sure, but where's Scooby? One minute we were sitting down for a Scooby Snack, and the next minute he was gone," Shaggy answered.

"Well, you found us instead," said Velma. "Now let's all try to find Fred and Scooby."

The three friends looked around the room for clues and Daphne spotted more of the purple goo seeping from under the bookcase. "Hey, look at this!"

Velma noticed that the bookcase had small hinges along one side. "It looks like a secret door. Help me push," she called to the others.

The bookcase spun around revealing Fred and Scooby on the other side. It also revealed someone else....

It was the hotel owner, Mr MacDuff, and he was all tied up! The gang quickly freed him.

"What happened?" Velma asked.

"A masked man grabbed me and took me down here," he explained.

Everyone looked around the lab for clues. In the centre of the room was a large hole.

"What's that?" Shaggy said as he peered into the hole.

"That's strange. It's more of that purple goo," began Velma. "Maybe we can use it to catch whoever's behind this ..."

"... sticky situation," finished Fred.

The gang took some of the purple goo from the lab and put it in different parts of the hotel.

Shaggy and Scooby headed back upstairs where they had first heard the moaning. This time, though, they lured out the mysterious stranger with – what else? A Scooby Snack!

According to plan, the masked figure chased Shaggy and Scooby down the hall, out of the window and towards the tower on the roof.

"Now!" yelled Fred.

Purple goo oozed out of the 'goo-goyles' on the roof, trapping the masked figure.

"Gotcha!" said Velma.

The gang brought the masked figure – now covered in goo – back into the hotel. Fred took off the figure's mask, and everyone gasped. It was Marty, the porter!

"Marty!" exclaimed Mr MacDuff. "How could you do this to me?"

Marty explained that a rich property developer had paid him a lot of money to make everyone think the hotel was haunted. Then Mr MacDuff would have to sell the mansion.

"He wanted to tear down the mansion to get to the goo below," explained Marty. "Apparently it's worth a fortune."

Mr MacDuff was stunned. "I had no idea."

"What will you do with the goo?" Fred asked Mr MacDuff.

But before he could answer, Shaggy interrupted. "Like, I think Scoob has some good ideas!"

"Scooby-Dooby Goo!" exclaimed Scooby, as everyone laughed.

THE END

TO THE MANSION

Scooby, Shaggy and the gang are heading to the Mystery Mansion to solve another case. Can you help them find the correct road and avoid dead ends?

Scooby is being chased by a mysterious monster! Join the dots to reveal the spookster.

Yikes! It's a

_____

SEARCH FOR THE MYSTERY MACHINE

Welcome to your very own Scooby-Doo treasure hunt!

YOU'LL NEED:

- **SOME FRIENDS** - enough to split into two teams
  (you can play this on your own, too, but it's much more fun with friends!)
- **A PAIR OF SCISSORS** - to cut out your game parts
- **A PEN OR PENCIL** - to write out your clues
- **SOME GLUE** - for building the Mystery Machine prize
- **AN ADULT** - to help with the above

HOW TO PLAY:

1. Carefully cut out your clue cards and magnifying glasses.
2. Ask an adult, or someone who is not taking part in the game, to write out the clue cards (on the blank side) and hide all of them around the house. Each clue should be a hint to where you can find the next clue.
   E.g. 'I'm in a very cold place' - the next clue would then be placed in the fridge.
3. Cut out and build the Mystery Machine, then ask the adult to hide it. The last clue should lead to where it is hidden and the first team to find it wins.
4. Split into two teams, each with a magnifying glass to search for clues. Remember, whoever finds the clues first should leave them in place for the following team to find, too.

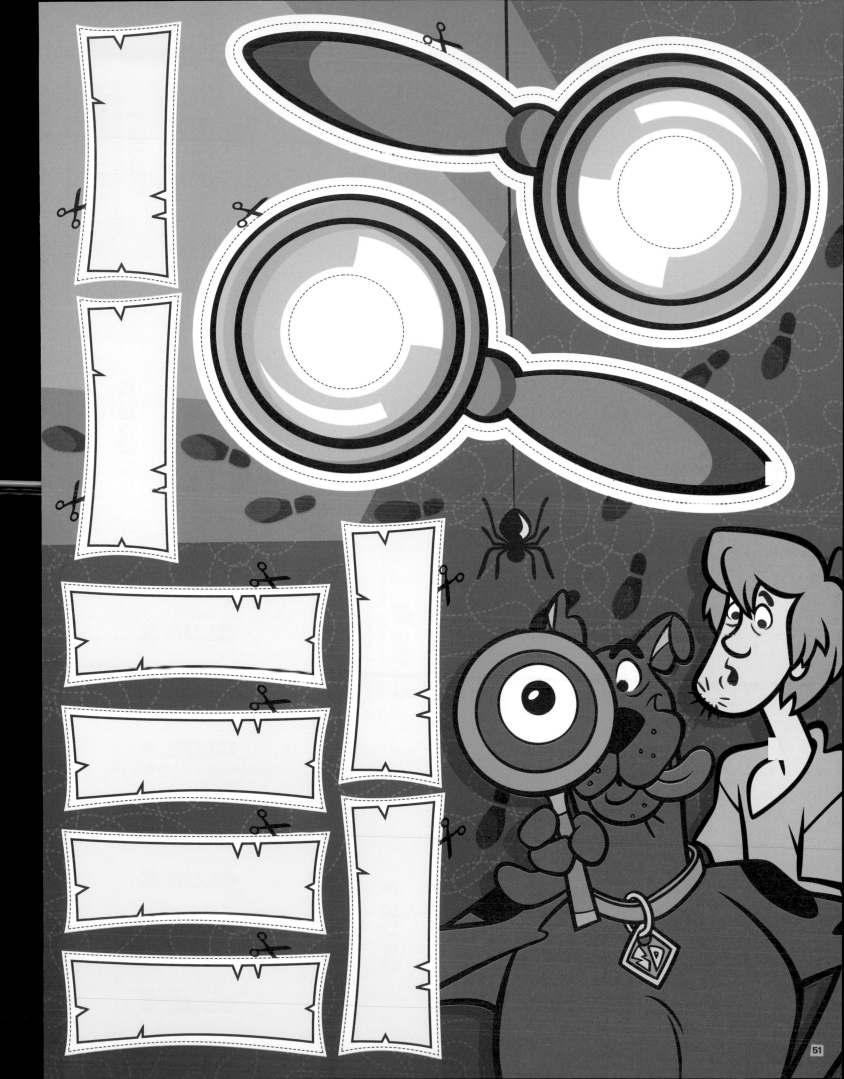

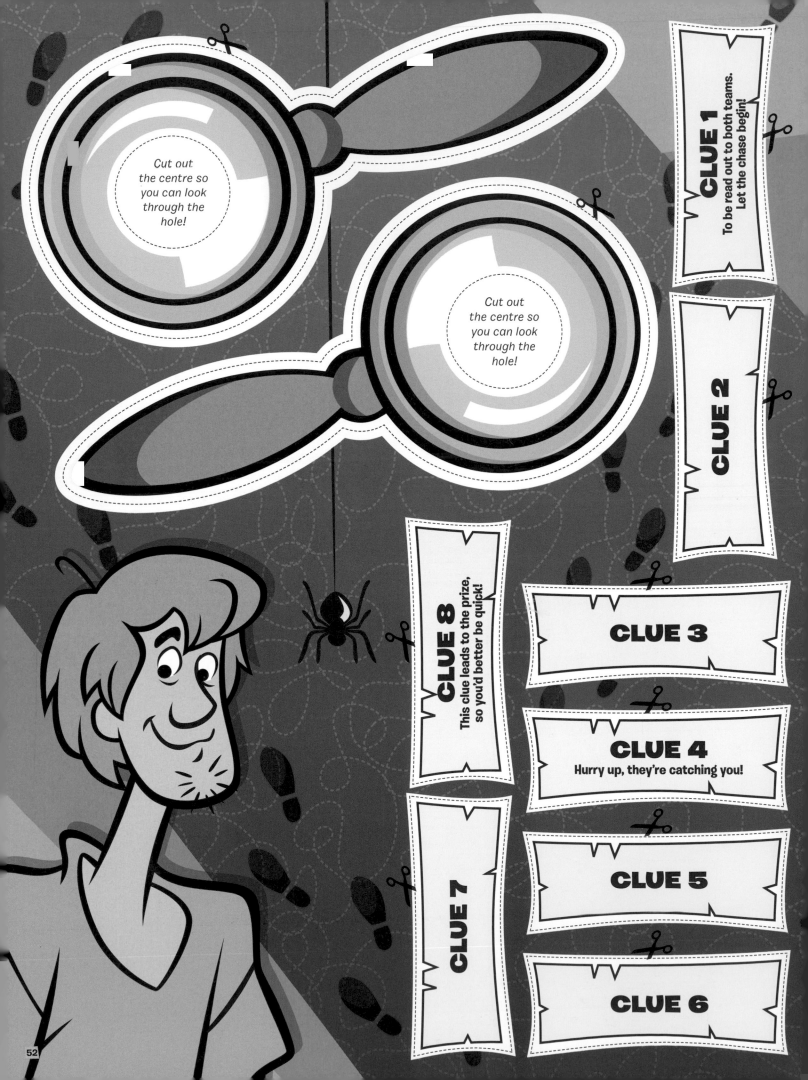

Cut out the centre so you can look through the hole!

Cut out the centre so you can look through the hole!

CLUE 1
To be read out to both teams. Let the chase begin!

CLUE 2

CLUE 3

CLUE 4
Hurry up, they're catching you!

CLUE 5

CLUE 6

CLUE 7

CLUE 8
This clue leads to the prize, so you'd better be quick!

MYSTERY MACHINE

The prize for the fastest team to find all the
clues is their very own mini Mystery Machine.
See the next page for instructions on cutting out
and folding it together, then ask an adult
to put it in the final hiding place.

HOW TO MAKE THE MYSTERY MACHINE:

1. Carefully cut out the Mystery Machine along the dotted line.
2. Fold in the tabs along each of the solid lines - be sure to fold tabs in towards the plain green side.
3. Once folded, glue the tabs, press into place and wait for it to dry. Then let the chase commence!

A HAIR-RAISING MYSTERY

Use the space below to write your very own mystery.
Scooby and the gang will help you solve it!

Think of the characters, and a place where your story will take place. Don't forget a fiendish villain, too - no Scooby story is complete without one!

CREEPY CREATURE

**Something's got Scooby seriously spooked!
Join the dots to reveal what it is.**

Colour in this picture of Scooby, Shaggy and the gang!

Scooby's SCARY Story time

Up, up and away!

It was Saturday night and the gang were trying to decide what to do.

Velma checked the newspaper.

"We can go to the car races at Simon's Speedway. Buy two admission tickets, get one free," she told them.

Shaggy peered over her shoulder and said, "Like, here's an even better deal at the Midnight Madness Balloon Race. Buy two pizzas, get one free."

"Rummy!" Scooby rubbed his growling stomach.

"It's the full moon special!" Daphne read on. "By the light of the moon, cheer on balloon-racing champ Swifty Malone, while dining under the stars at our Sky High Snack Stand."

"I'll get the Mystery Machine," Fred said. "Let's go!"

At the fair, Fred circled the car park trying to find a space. "It's really crowded," he sighed. "This could take a while."

Shaggy and Scooby hopped out of the van.

"No problem," Shaggy told the others. "Scoob and I will get some food. Six pizzas." He looked at his friends. "Anything for you guys?"

Shaggy and Scooby hurried through the swarm of people.

They passed signs saying 'Go Swifty!' and booths filled with souvenirs. Hot-air balloons hovered everywhere, tethered to the ground.

"Here! Everyone! Take one!" A man pushed past them, handing out fliers for Simon's Speedway. "Go to the Speedway!" he told Shaggy. "Trust me, it's a lot more fun than this place."

"Like, I don't know what he's talking about," Shaggy shouted to Scooby above the noise. "This place is jumping."

But when Shaggy and Scooby got to the Sky High Snack Stand, they were the only ones there.

"Hey, what's going on?" Shaggy said.

"I'm closing up," said Skye, the owner. She peered around the fair nervously and lowered her voice. "It's so scary. There's a werewolf on the loose!"

Shaggy trembled with fear. "What? No pizza? Now *that's* scary."

Just then, Fred and the rest of the gang caught up with Shaggy and Scooby. "What's going on? Why is everyone leaving?" asked Fred.

"There's no food!" cried Shaggy. "And there's a werewolf!"

"Werewolf?" Daphne repeated.

"There, wolf." Skye pointed to the dark woods. "And there." She nodded towards the lake and finish line. "He has been spotted everywhere! Swifty's telling people to drop out of the race for their own safety. Everyone's going home."

"Jinkies!" said Velma. "Perhaps we can help. Guys, let's take a look around and see if we can spot any clues."

The gang roamed around the fair.

"Look!" said Daphne, peering at the dirt. "Are those werewolf tracks?"

The animal prints led to the car park, right by the Mystery Machine.

"Maybe they're just Scooby's tracks." Daphne was disappointed. "And they look strange because people have been stepping on them."

"Or maybe not," Velma murmured.

Next, the gang circled closer to the woods. Suddenly, a chilling wind began to blow and papers flew everywhere. *Awhoooo!* A howling sound rang out.

"Rind?" asked Scooby, hopefully.

"Like, that's no wind," said Shaggy as a dark shape streaked through the woods. "It's the werewolf!"

"We need someone to lure the werewolf out into the open," Fred said.

Everyone turned to look at Shaggy and Scooby.

"Guys, would you help us trap the werewolf?" asked Velma.

"Ro ray," said Scooby.

"No way," Shaggy agreed.

"For a Scooby Snack?" Velma added.

"Like, not even for a whole box of Scooby Snacks," Shaggy declared.

"How about some burgers?" asked Velma.

Skye quickly threw some burgers on the grill just for Shaggy and Scooby.

"Oh, Mr Werewolf," Shaggy called in a small, shaky voice. "Here we are, not trying to catch you or anything."

Awhoooo! Shaggy and Scooby spun round. The werewolf stood on a large rock, just a few metres away, howling at the moon. A beam of light glinted off his long, sharp teeth.

"Zoinks!" shouted Shaggy. "Let's get out of here."

The friends ran through the fair. The werewolf followed closely behind them.

"Over here, Scoob!" Shaggy pulled Scooby-Doo over to a photo booth. They ducked behind a life size cut-out of old-time hot-air balloon pilots.

"Say cheese!" said the photographer, snapping a picture.

"Reez!" said Scooby.

The camera flashed.

AWHOOOO! Frightened by the sudden burst of light, the werewolf howled even louder. Shaggy and Scooby quickly scrambled to the next booth. They dived into a giant box of souvenir baseball caps.

So did the werewolf.

"Ruh-oh!" said Scooby. He and Shaggy jumped out.

"Come on, Scoob!" Shaggy said, racing towards the hot-air balloons that were waiting to lift off. "We'll lose him by the starting line!" The two hopped into a basket, and hid in its shadows.

Meanwhile, an announcer was about to call for the race to begin. "Swifty won't have much competition," he said. "Looks like the other racers have dropped out. But here goes anyway. Ready! Set!"

"Wait!" called a worker, standing beside Shaggy and Scooby's balloon. "This one has pilots!" She loosened the anchor rope.

"GO!" shouted the announcer.

"Yikes!" said Shaggy. "We're going for a ride."

The werewolf lunged for the basket, but it was too late. Shaggy and Scooby were already floating away.

"Can't catch us now!" said Shaggy.

The werewolf quickly leaped into another balloon. He pulled up the rope, taking off after Scooby and Shaggy. It was a hot-air balloon chase!

Shaggy and Scooby had to get away – and fast! They groped at the controls.

"Like, how do you work this thing?" Shaggy cried. He twisted a handle with all his strength. The burner flame shot up. For a second, nothing happened.

Then, suddenly, the balloon soared straight up in the air, jerking and bucking like a wild animal.

"Hang on!" shouted Shaggy. He twisted the handle the other way, but they kept going up. Shaggy gulped. "There's no way to steer!"

Even worse, the werewolf was gaining on them. They could see his bloodshot eyes. In a panic, Shaggy and Scooby shuffled to the far end of the basket.

"Hey look!" Shaggy said. "The gang's waiting for us at the finish line!"

Across the lake, Velma, Fred and Daphne stood next to the Mystery Machine, waving up at them.

"Man, if only we knew how to land," Shaggy moaned.

Suddenly, the werewolf leaned closer. Trying to reach Shaggy and Scooby, he swiped at the balloon. *Riiiip!* The fabric tore open. The balloon hissed, letting out air. Shaggy and Scooby began to drop, slowly at first, then faster and faster over the lake.

The balloon sank lower, skimming over the water. Waves lapped into the basket.

"Like, I wish I brought my swimming trunks," said Shaggy. They dropped even lower. Shaggy grabbed onto Scooby.

"Better hold your breath, Scoob! I think we're going for a dip."

All at once, the wind blew harder, pushing the balloon to shore – right past the finish line. Shaggy and Scooby bumped to a stop.

Above them, the werewolf howled in frustration. He climbed to the edge of the basket, ready to spring. In a flash, Fred leaped into the Mystery Machine and pressed a button. The van opened in the back. A cannon, mounted on one end, swung in the werewolf's direction.

The werewolf dived from the basket. The cannon fired. *Swish!* A net shot out and dropped over the werewolf. He somersaulted to the ground, wrapped in the trap. Daphne and Velma opened up a cage, and the werewolf rolled right in. The girls snapped the cage door shut.

"You got him!" said Shaggy, as he and Scooby raced over. "Now what?"

"We take off the mask!" Velma reached through the bars and pulled off the disguise. It was Simon, the Speedway owner!

"He wanted to scare everyone away from the balloon races, so they'd go to his car race instead!" Velma explained. "That's why the fliers were by the woods. And those tracks led to Simon's car, not the Mystery Machine!"

Simon gazed sadly at the crowds returning to the fair. "It would have worked, too, if it wasn't for you meddling kids."

Just then another balloon landed, and Swifty climbed out. "Did I win?" he asked.

The announcer shook his head. "Sorry, Swifty. But these meddling kids – I mean these racers – came in first."

"And they get the grand prize!" the announcer continued. "All the pizza they can eat."

Everyone was happy. Now Skye's snack stand couldn't close. It had to stay open ... and open ... and open....

THE END

BEAT THE WEREWOLF

Shaggy and Scooby are in a hot-air balloon being chased by a werewolf! Can you guide the terrified twosome through the clouds to meet the rest of the gang, safely on the ground?

START

FINISH

DARING DIFFERENCES

Can you spot and circle 10 differences between these two pictures?

Can you find all these words in the hot-air balloon above?

Scooby	**Werewolf**	**Claws**	**Balloon**	**Clouds**
Shaggy	**Growl**	**Howl**	**Basket**	**Escape**
Scared	**Teeth**	**Moonlight**	**Floating**	**Chase**

SPOOKY SPINNER

Want to see two pictures mysteriously blend into one? It's totally spook-tacular! Look at the next page for instructions to make these spinners.

SPINNER 1

SPINNER 2

65

HOW TO MAKE THE SPOOKY SPINNERS:

1. Cut out the discs, then fold them in half and glue the blank sides together.
2. Make a hole in both ends and insert a piece of string through each.
3. Twist the string between your fingers so the discs spin.

Make a hole here

Fold here

Make a hole here

Make a hole here

Fold here

Make a hole here

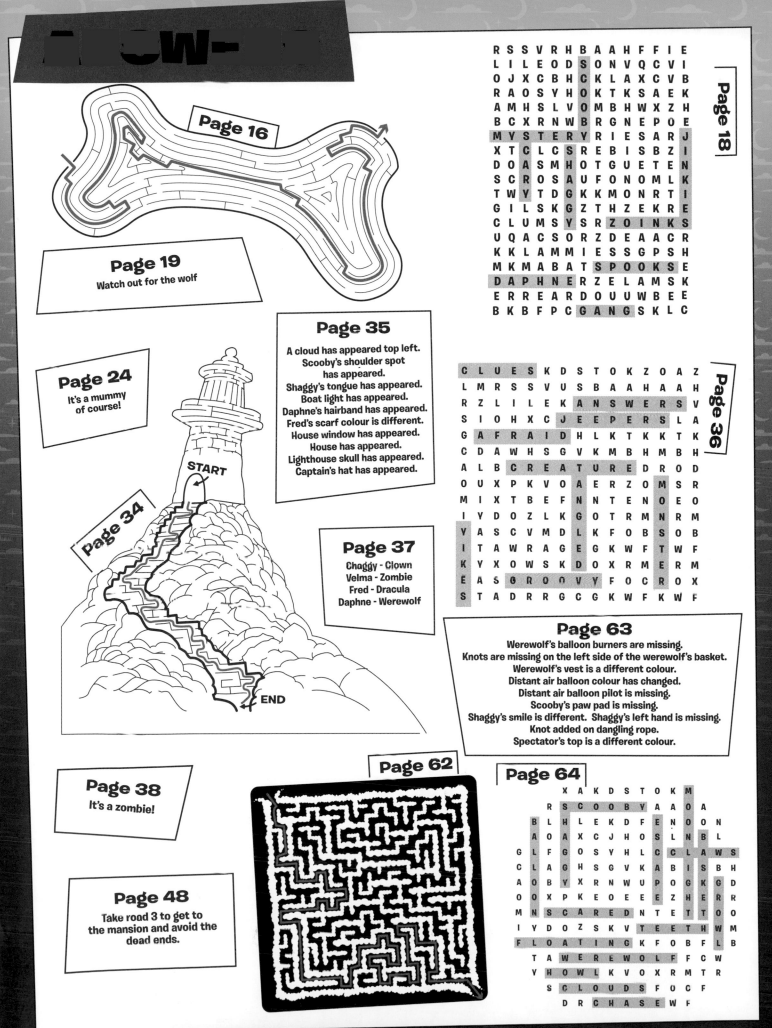

ANSWERS (title banner, top left)

Page 16

Page 19
Watch out for the wolf

Page 24
It's a mummy of course!

Page 34

Page 35
A cloud has appeared top left.
Scooby's shoulder spot has appeared.
Shaggy's tongue has appeared.
Boat light has appeared.
Daphne's hairband has appeared.
Fred's scarf colour is different.
House window has appeared.
House has appeared.
Lighthouse skull has appeared.
Captain's hat has appeared.

START

END

Page 37
Chaggy - Clown
Velma - Zombie
Fred - Dracula
Daphne - Werewolf

Page 38
It's a zombie!

Page 48
Take road 3 to get to the mansion and avoid the dead ends.

Page 62

Page 18

```
R S S V R H B A A H F F I E
L I L E O D S O N V Q C V I
O J X C B H C K L A X C V B
R A O S V H O K T K S A E K
A M H S L V O M B H W X Z H
B C X R N W B R G N E P O E
M Y S T E R Y R I E S A R J
X T C L C S R E B I S B Z I
D O A S M H O T G U E T E N
S C R O S A U F O N O M L K
T W Y T D G K K M O N R T I
G I L S K G Z T H Z E K R E
C L U M S Y S R Z O I N K S
U Q A C S O R Z D E A A C R
K K L A M M I E S S G P S H
M K M A B A T S P O O K S E
D A P H N E R Z E L A M S K
E R R E A R D O U U W B E E
B K B F P C G A N G S K L C
```

Page 36

```
C L U E S K D S T O K Z O A Z
L M R S S V U S B A A H A A H
R Z L I L E K A N S W E R S V
S I O H X C J E E P E R S L A
G A F R A I D H L K T K K T K
C D A W H S G V K M B H M B H
A L B C R E A T U R E D R O D
O U X P K V O A E R Z O M S R
M I X T B E F N N T E N O E O
I Y D O Z L K G O T R M N R M
V A S C V M D L K F O B S O B
I T A W R A G E G K W F T W F
K V X O W S K D O X R M E R M
E A S G R O O V Y F O C R O X
S T A D R R G C G K W F K W F
```

Page 63
Werewolf's balloon burners are missing.
Knots are missing on the left side of the werewolf's basket.
Werewolf's vest is a different colour.
Distant air balloon colour has changed.
Distant air balloon pilot is missing.
Scooby's paw pad is missing.
Shaggy's smile is different. Shaggy's left hand is missing.
Knot added on dangling rope.
Spectator's top is a different colour.

Page 64

```
        X A K D S T O K M
    R S C O O B Y A A O A
  B L H L E K D F E N O N
  A O A X C J H O S L N L
G L F G O S Y H L C C L A W S
C L A G H S G V K A B I S B H
A O B V X R N W U P O G K G D
O O X P K E O E E Z H E O R O
M N S C A R E D N T E T T O M
I Y D O Z L K G O T T E E T H
F L O A T I N G K F O B F B
T A W E R E W O L F F C W
V H O W L K V O X R M T R
  S C L O U D S F O C F
    D R C H A S E W F
```